The Land Under Your Feet

A New Found Friend

Written by
Clifford Smith and Judi Sarkisian
Illustrated by Clifford Smith
Original Songs and Arrangements by Jeff Pekarek

To Ezra!
I hope you enjoy
your "new found friend" and
many many more!
Love,
Judi Sarkisian

AuthorHouse™
1663 Liberty Drive, Suite 200
Bloomington, IN 47403
www.authorhouse.com
Phone: 1-800-839-8640

AuthorHouse™ UK Ltd.
500 Avebury Boulevard
Central Milton Keynes, MK9 2BE
www.authorhouse.co.uk
Phone: 08001974150

First published by AuthorHouse 4/5/2006

ISBN: 1-4259-1389-X (sc)

Printed in the United States of America
Bloomington, Indiana

This book is printed on acid-free paper.

Bloomington, IN Milton Keynes, UK

authorHOUSE"

A lone space traveler from a very, very small planet was preparing for his long journey to Earth. Did I say very small? This planet was so small, it had never been seen by any stargazer in the world, until now. This is the first adventure of Spencer Higgins, the little boy who discovered the planet, his dog, Crackers and the space traveler, Gumbubble.

Chapter 1

About a week ago, while watching the stars, Spencer noticed a misty orange spot on his telescope lens. He quickly grabbed a handkerchief from his pocket to wipe the lens clean. When Spencer resumed his gazing, he noticed that the spot was still there. Could it be possible that he had discovered an unknown planet? He stared intently through his telescope. He thought he saw a shooting star go by the misty orange planet.

"Spencer, time for dinner," called his mother. Scientist Spencer was in the middle of a great discovery. He had no time for dinner.

"In a minute, Mom."

"No, now!" she said.

While Spencer was having dinner, the shooting star continued toward Earth. It was actually a space traveler streaking across space, in search of a planet like his home planet, Retuo Ecaps. Flying through space, dodging asteroids and slipping through space dust, he made his way closer and closer to Earth.

Chapter 2

Spencer hurriedly finished his dinner so he could return to his telescope. He asked his mother if he could go back outside.

"Is your homework finished?" she asked.

"Not really Mom," he replied.

"Finish your homework first," she said.
Scientific discovery would have to wait; Spencer and his dog Crackers reluctantly   went upstairs to finish Spencer's homework.

Meanwhile, out in space, the lone space traveler had a lot of work ahead of him. Maneuvering through Earth's atmosphere and landing the spaceship safely wasn't easy. The gradual descent to Earth was very bumpy. The spaceman landed his spaceship with a ***BANG! CRASH! BOOM****!* right on the grassy field behind Cracker's doghouse in Spencer's backyard.

It was difficult for Spencer to do his homework, he kept thinking of his discovery of the misty orange planet. He wished he had written down the coordinates of the planet according to the star-maps.

Later that evening, when everyone else was sleeping, Spencer and Crackers crept downstairs to see if what they saw was really real. To his dismay, Spencer could not find the planet again. Frustrated and a little sad, he and Crackers went back upstairs to bed.

Chapter 4

The next morning when Spencer woke up he remembered his science project was due. He needed 20 ordinary yard bugs, fast! He jumped out of bed and dashed downstairs with a jar.

"Mom, I'll be back in a minute for breakfast. I need some bugs for my science project," Spencer shouted.

Spencer and Crackers headed for the backyard to look for bugs.

Crackers was a very good bug finder and soon the jar was buzzing with bugs. All of a sudden, Crackers began to BARK and BARK. He had his paw on a very strange bug! It was a silver blue thing in the grass, about the size of a shoe box, and it had a strange hum coming from it.

When Crackers sniffed the thing, something went up his nose and he began to sneeze, *ACHoooo! AAACHoooo!* Spencer raced over to see why Crackers was barking and sneezing.

When Spencer saw the silver thing, the look on his face was like it was his birthday. He carefully reached for the thing. It was very heavy. Then he and Crackers heard a strange whirring and clicking sound behind them. Slowly, they turned around to see what it was.

Spencer the Schoolboy

Jeff Basile Pekarek

Chapter 5

Spencer and Crackers couldn't believe their eyes. They rubbed their eyes and looked again. It didn't change what they saw. Right behind them stood a little man about 3 inches tall. He had his hands on his hips and was looking straight at them.

Spencer tried to warn Crackers to stay back, but his dog was already busy sniffing the little green and yellow spotted man. Crackers sneezed again and rubbed his nose on the ground.

Crackers felt a tingle all over his body and then he thought he could hear the little man say, "where am I, who are you, what are you?"

When he tried to answer he found he could talk to the spaceman, "I am Crackers, I'm a dog and you are on our land."

Right then Spencer's Mom called them for breakfast. Not even a space traveler could keep Crackers from eating. As he took off running toward the house, Spencer snatched the little spaceman up and put him in his shirt pocket, along with the jar of bugs.

Chapter 6

Breakfast was barely finished when it was time for school. The bus driver was already out front waiting, *HONK HOOOOONK!* Spencer raced upstairs to get his backpack.

He put the little man in his sock drawer, turned to Crackers and said, "watch him and don't let him out of your sight." Then off he ran to school.

Crackers crept up to the sock drawer. He wasn't sure what the little man would do to him. He carefully peeked inside. Crackers couldn't see anything in the dark sock drawer.

Then he heard, "hello, what are you?"

"I am a dog," he replied, "what and who are you?"

"I am the spaceman who gave you the gift of speech. Everything on my planet can speak."

"Spaceman, does that mean you're from another planet?" Crackers asked.

"Smart dog," the spaceman replied.

Crackers asked the spaceman why he had come to their back yard, but the only response he got was the whirring and clicking sound.

Chapter 7

When Spencer goes to school he is gone a long time, in "dog" time, so Crackers got to know a lot about their newfound friend.

The little man leaped out of the drawer and began looking, touching and asking about everything in Spencer's room.

Crackers followed closely with his nose re-examining everything the spaceman touched. He kept asking the little man, "why are you here, what do you want? And what's your name?" Finally the spaceman put his hands up and said to Crackers, "slow down, slow down."

"All of your questions will be answered, but first things first. My name is Gipiyitipititipop."

"Huh?" said Crackers. "That is too hard for a dog to say. You look like that stuff Spencer chews and blows bubbles with." Crackers looked closely at the spaceman and said, "I'm calling you Gumbubble."

The little man looked puzzled. "Whatever," he replied.

Crackers asked him again, "why have you come here?"

Gumbubble leaped up on Crackers' nose and staring into his eyes said, "this land has all the things my people like. I came here to take it over."

Crackers was very shocked and upset to find out about this plan. "You can't do that! You're too little to take over this land."

"Wait a minute! What do you mean I'm too little to take over? I'm the tallest man on my planet." He whirred and clicked loudly. "The powers I have make me a giant. Didn't I give you the gift of speech?"

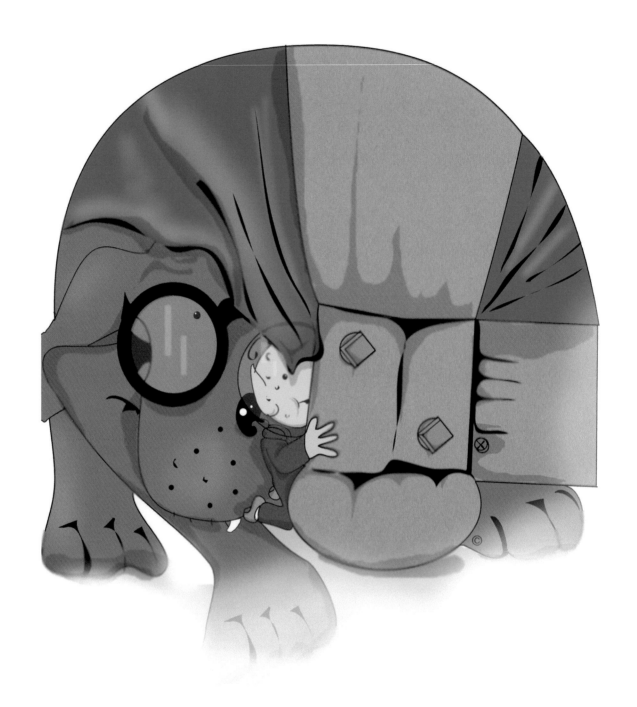

Chapter 8

The front door slammed with a big bang. The loud bang scared Gumbubble so much, he hid under the bed. "It's just Spencer coming home from school," Crackers said.

"School? What's school?" Gumbubble asked curiously.

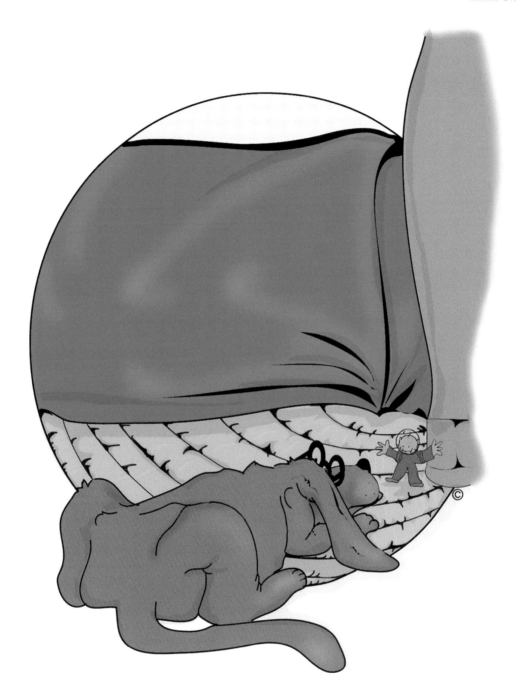

Crackers climbed under the bed next to Gumbubble. He was surprised Gumbubble didn't know what school was. Why, even dogs know about school! "That is where kids and puppies learn about how to be grown up."

"Very interesting," Gumbubble said, "but odd. I was born just like I am."

The bedroom door burst open and Spencer came running in. He pulled out the sock drawer looking for his new found friend. Frantically, Spencer pulled everything out of the drawer, but he couldn't find the little spaceman.

Then Spencer heard from under the bed, "who are you?"

Spencer looked under the bed and came eye to eye with the little man. He stuttered, "my…my name is Spencer Higgins, who are you?"

Crackers started to explain who the little man was, and was surprised to hear that when he talked to Spencer, he still talked dog talk. He was a little sad; he hoped he would be able to talk to Spencer like he talked to the spaceman.

Gumbubble hopped on Spencer's shoulder and told him everything he had told the dog. Crackers began to shiver when he repeated that he had come to take over the earth. Crackers was surprised when he saw that Spencer did not seem too upset about the spaceman's plan to take over *THEIR* land.

Gumbubble's Song

Jeff Basile Pekarek

Chapter 9

Spencer gently picked up the little man and sat on the bed. "You can't take over our land, it already belongs to us. This land is America, the home of the free and the brave! And besides, why do you want to take it over?"

Gumbubble whirred and clicked softly, "because you have so many things we like and don't have! And besides when I flew my spaceship I saw lots of land that was just sitting there with no one on it. If I can't have your land, I will just take that other land!"

Spencer grew very serious. He could see that it was not going to be easy to explain to Gumbubble that he could not do whatever he wanted to do. Now Spencer began to be concerned, what if the little spaceman really could take over the land! He would have to convince Gumbubble to go back to his own planet to live.

Chapter 10

"Aha." Spencer said. "I bet I can explain it by telling you about the American flag." He took down the flag that was over his desk. "This flag is our official national symbol of the United States of America," he said proudly.

"The red and white stripes represent the original 13 colonies and the white stars on

the blue field represent the 50 states that exist now. Even the colors are important.

White stands for Purity and Innocence; Red is for Hardiness and Valor and the Blue is for Vigilance, Perseverance and Justice.

Americans put their flag up over their land to remind everyone that it belongs to them."

Gumbubble whirred and clicked, "these are very good things, but I still want to take over your land for my people. And besides, you said this is the land of the free, what is it to be free? Doesn't that mean you can do anything you want to? And I want to take over your land!" Gumbubble started hopping up and down.

Spencer needed help. If he didn't convince the spaceman that he could not take over the land, the whole earth might be in danger.

Spencer picked up his dictionary. "Look here," he said, holding the dictionary in front of Gumbubble.

"This is what free means to Americans, see it says:

To be free is to have the right to speak, assemble, petition, vote and NOT to be under the control of some other person or foreign government.

In this land each person is the government."

Gumbubble stopped whirring and clicking, he sat down on the dictionary. Crackers came over and watched Spencer watching Gumbubble's reply. "But I like it here! I know everyone from my planet would like it here!"

Spencer looked very sad. This was not good.

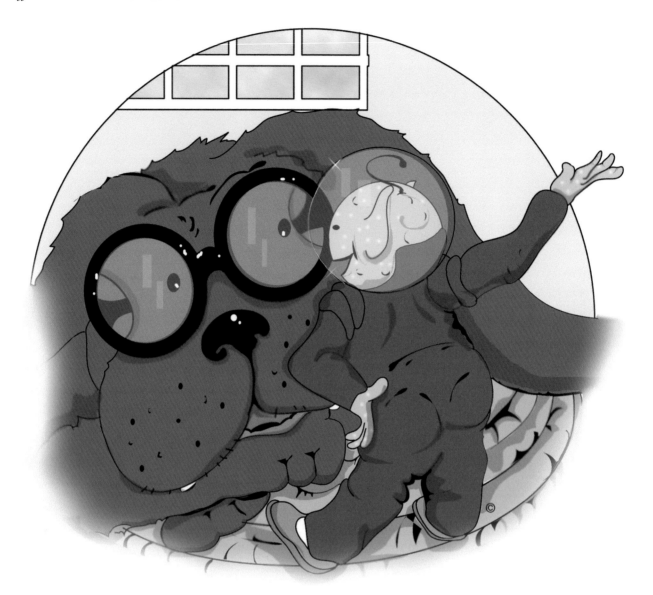

Then Crackers had the best idea he had ever had!
He leaned over to the little spaceman and whispered,
"VACATION! Ask Spencer to explain *'vacation'* to you."
"What about a *vacation*?" Gumbubble asked Spencer.

Spencer's face lit up. *"VACATION!* That's a super idea! You go home and bring your family and friends here for a vacation. Vacations are the most fun of all. You go to someone else's land and go camping, go to amusement parks, watch fireworks, go river rafting and enjoy everything the land has to offer. But you can't have a vacation here if you take over the land."

Gumbubble began hopping up and down and clicking excitedly, "*VACATION*! That is much better than taking over the land! I must go back to tell my people to start planning their *vacations*." Crackers and Spencer both gave a big sigh of relief. They had done it. They had saved their land.

Now they could really enjoy their new found friend. In no time at all they were busy finding gifts for Gumbubble to take back to his family and friends. Later that night, as they watched his little spaceship take off across the sky, they hoped they would see him again.

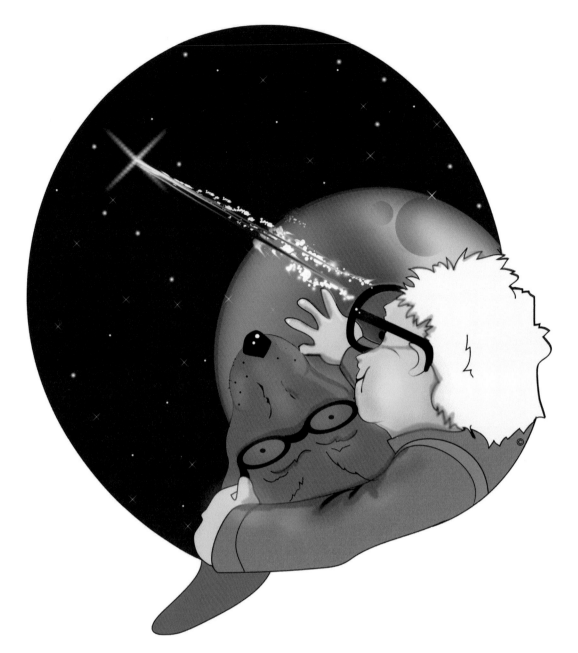

Crackers had really enjoyed being able to talk to the little spaceman. He sighed and leaned close to Spencer. Maybe when Gumbubble returned he would make it so Crackers could talk to Spencer.

Wait and see.

Gumbubble raced his ship through the night sky toward his home planet with thoughts of friends, family and the love of his home.

Gumbubble knew he would return to earth with his family on his vacation. Visit Gumbubble and his family in the next episode, Gumbubble Goes on Vacation.

See you then, but have you checked your backyard today?

The Land Under Your Feet

Jeff Basile Pekarek

There is something of yours which is al - so something of mine
If you don't have a piece then you still have part of the whole

This is something worth more than a - ny trea-sure that you can find
If you're rich or you're poor you are still a part of it's soul

You can have your own piece but you can - not have the whole thing and
Peo-ple from eve - ry where come to make the mystery com- plete this

you can do your own thing in the place of which I sing!
won - der of which I sing is the land un - der your feet!

CPSIA information can be obtained
at www.ICGtesting.com
Printed in the USA
BVIC01n0939101014
370174BV00003B/3